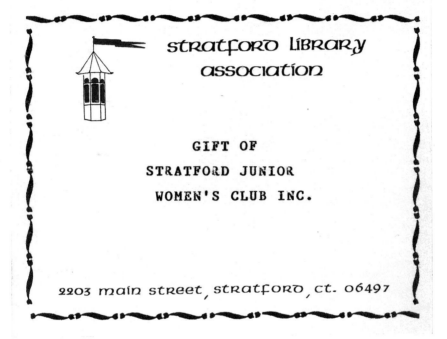

# YOUNG CAM JANSEN
## and the
## Dinosaur Game

A Viking Easy-to-Read

by David A. Adler

illustrated by Susanna Natti

**VIKING**

VIKING
Published by the Penguin Group
Penguin Books USA Inc., 375 Hudson Street, New York, New York 10014, U.S.A.
Penguin Books Ltd, 27 Wrights Lane, London W8 5TZ, England
Penguin Books Australia Ltd, Ringwood, Victoria, Australia
Penguin Books Canada Ltd, 10 Alcorn Avenue, Toronto, Ontario, Canada M4V 3B2
Penguin Books (N.Z.) Ltd, 182-190 Wairau Road, Auckland 10, New Zealand

Penguin Books Ltd, Registered Offices: Harmondsworth, Middlesex, England

First published in 1996 by Viking, a division of Penguin Books USA Inc.

1   3   5   7   9   10   8   6   4   2

Text copyright © David A. Adler, 1996
Illustrations copyright © Susanna Natti, 1996
All rights reserved

LIBRARY OF CONGRESS CATALOGING-IN-PUBLICATION DATA
Adler, David A.
Young Cam Jansen and the dinosaur game / by David A. Adler ;
pictures by Susanna Natti.    p.   cm.—(A Viking easy-to-read)
Summary: When eight-year-old sleuth Cam Jansen and her
friend Eric go to a birthday party, she uses her photographic memory
to solve the puzzle of the dinosaur count.
ISBN 0-670-86399-8 (hc)
[1. Mystery and detective stories  2. Parties—Fiction.]
I. Natti, Susanna, ill. II. Title. III. Series.
PZ7.A2615Yo  1996  [Fic]—dc20  95-46463  CIP  AC

Printed in Singapore
Set in Bookman

Reading Level 1.7

# CONTENTS

# 1. I'M GOING! I'M GOING!

Honk! Honk!

"I'm going! I'm going!"

Mr. Jansen said.

He was driving his daughter Cam

and her friend Eric Shelton

to a birthday party.

Mr. Jansen stopped at the corner.

He looked at the street signs.

4

Then he said, "I'm sorry.

I forgot where the party is.

And I forgot to bring the invitation."

Honk! Honk!

"I'm going! I'm going!"

Mr. Jansen said as he drove on.

"But I don't know where I'm going."

Mr. Jansen drove to the next corner
and parked the car.

Eric said, "I'm sure Cam remembers
where the party is."

Cam closed her eyes and said, "Click!"
Cam always closes her eyes
and says "Click!" when she wants
to remember something.

Cam has an amazing memory.

"My memory is like a camera," she says.

"I have a picture in my head

of everything I've seen.

'Click!' is the sound my camera makes."

Cam's real name is Jennifer.

But because of her great memory,

people started to call her "the Camera."

Then "the Camera" became just Cam.

"I'm looking at the invitation,"

Cam said, with her eyes closed.

"It says, 'Come to a party

for Jane Bell. 3:00 p.m.,

86 Robin Lane.'"

Cam opened her eyes.

Mr. Jansen drove to 86 Robin Lane.

There were balloons

and a big HAPPY BIRTHDAY sign

on the front door.

Mr. Bell opened the door and said,

"Come in. Come in."

He pointed to a big jar.

"Before you join the others,

guess how many dinosaurs are in this jar.

Remember your guess.

The best one wins the dinosaurs."

The jar was filled with

blue, green, yellow, and red toy dinosaurs.

Next to the jar were slips of paper,

a few pens, and a shoe box.

Cam tried to count the dinosaurs.

But she couldn't.

Lots of dinosaurs were hidden

behind other dinosaurs.

Cam wrote her guess

on a slip of paper.

She put the paper in the shoe box.

Eric looked at the jar.

He looked for a long time.

Then he wrote his guess

on a slip of paper, too.

He put the paper in the shoe box.

Eric said, "I hope I win."

Then Cam and Eric went to the kitchen.

Their friends were there,

sitting around the table.

# 2. THE DINOSAUR GAME

Mrs. Bell said, "Good, everyone is here.

I'll get the birthday cake."

She carried a large cake to the table.

The cake was covered

with chocolate icing.

Mrs. Bell lit the candles.

Everyone sang "Happy Birthday."

Then Mrs. Bell gave each child

a piece of birthday cake.

They were all eating cake

when Mr. Bell walked into the room.

"I counted the dinosaurs," he said.

"There were 154 in the jar."

Mr. Bell took a large piece

of birthday cake.

Eric said, "I guessed 150.

Maybe I'll win."

Rachel said, "I guessed 300."

"Who won?" Jane asked.

"Who won the dinosaur game?"

Mr. Bell smiled.

"We'll see," he said,

"as soon as I finish eating."

Some children took a second piece of cake.

Some went into the den to play.

When Mr. Bell finished,

he brought in the shoe box.

He turned it over and picked up

a slip of paper.

"180," he read.

Then he showed it to everyone.

"That was my guess," Jane said.

One by one Mr. Bell read the guesses.

"100 . . . 300 . . . 1,000 . . . 450 . . . 200."

Cam said, "200 was my guess."

Mr. Bell looked at the next slip of paper.

He read, "150."

"That was my guess," Eric said.

Then Mr. Bell held up the last slip of paper
and read, "154."

"That's mine," Robert said. "I win."

"You <u>do</u> win," Mr. Bell said.

"You guessed the exact number.

And here's your prize."

He gave Robert the jar of dinosaurs.

Cam looked at Robert.

Then she looked at the slip of paper

in Mr. Bell's hand and said, "Click!"

Eric whispered to Cam,

"That's amazing.

He guessed the exact number

of dinosaurs."

"Yes," Cam said. "It is amazing.

It's almost <u>too</u> amazing."

## 3. CLICK!

Robert spilled the dinosaurs

onto the table.

"They're cute," Rachel said.

"Can I have one?" Jason asked.

Rachel asked, "Can I have one, too?"

"I'm not giving them away," Robert said.

"I'm selling them."

"I want a red one," Rachel said.

"I'll give you the money

at school tomorrow."

"I want three green dinosaurs

and two yellows," Jason said.

Mrs. Bell said,

"Let's play another guessing game."

She held up a small box.

"I have something in here.

It has a face and it runs.

What is it?"

"Does it run fast?" Rachel asked.

Mrs. Bell said, "I hope not."

Eric asked, "Does it have eight legs?

Is it a spider?"

Mrs. Bell said, "It doesn't have any legs."

Cam asked, "Does it have hands?

Is it a watch?"

Cam was right.

Mr. Bell said,

"Now let's play musical chairs."

He set six chairs in a line.

He turned on some music.

Then Mr. Bell told the children,

"Walk around the chairs.

When the music stops, sit down.

Whoever can't find a seat

is out of the game."

The children walked around the chairs.

But not Cam.

She looked at the chairs.

She counted them.

Then she closed her eyes

and said, "Click!"

# 4. YOU MADE ME LOSE

The music stopped.

Everyone but Cam sat down.

She was out of the game.

Mr. Bell took one chair away and

turned on the music again.

Cam opened her eyes.

She went over to the table.

She looked at the

slips of paper.

Then, as Eric walked past,

she whispered to him,

"I have something to show you."

Eric turned, and the music stopped.

Everyone but Eric sat down.

He was out of the game.

Mr. Bell took one chair away

and turned on the music again.

When Robert walked past

Cam whispered to him,

"And I have something to show you."

Robert turned, and the music stopped.

Everyone but Robert sat down.

Robert was out of the game.

He told Cam,

"You made me lose at musical chairs."

Cam said, "And I'll make you lose

the dinosaurs, too."

Cam said to Robert, "You wrote 154

<u>after</u> Jane's father counted the dinosaurs."

"I did not!" Robert said.

Cam told him, "Mr. Bell turned over

the shoe box.

The papers fell out upside down.

They fell out in the same order

they were put in.

Jane's guess was first.

Eric and I were the last
to come to the party.

Our guesses should have been last.

But yours was."

Robert said, "Maybe the papers got mixed up."

Cam told him, "There were eight guesses

but only seven kids are at the party.

You guessed twice.

You guessed when you came to the party.

You guessed again

after Jane's father told us

there were 154 dinosaurs in the jar."

"I did not," Robert said.

Cam picked up Robert's winning guess.

"And look at this," she said.

Cam pointed to a chocolate smudge.

"You wrote this

after we had birthday cake.

That's why there's chocolate on it."

Cam and Eric looked at Robert's hands.

There was chocolate on them, too.

Robert looked down.

"You're right," he said softly.

"My real guess was 1,000 dinosaurs."

Robert put the dinosaurs back in the jar.

After the game of musical chairs ended,

Robert talked to Mrs. Bell.

He told her that Eric had really won

the dinosaur game.

Mrs. Bell gave the jar to Eric.

Rachel said, "I want to buy a red dinosaur."

Jason said, "I want three green dinosaurs

and two yellows."

Eric told them, "I'm not selling the dinosaurs.

I'm sharing them."

The children sat in a circle.

Eric walked around them.

"One for you," he said

as he gave each child a dinosaur.

"And one for you. And one for you."

After Eric had given everyone else a dinosaur

he put one on an empty chair and said,

"And one for me."

Eric walked around the circle

again and again.

He walked around until

the big jar of toy dinosaurs was empty.